Succubus With Benefits

A Femdom Monster Girl Erotica

Cithrel

Contents

1. Hunger   1

2. Heat   9

3. Bystander   14

4. Taste   21

5. Feast   32

6. Dream   37

About the Author   40

Join the Newsletter   41

Also by Cithrel   42

1

Hunger

It *was* good to be alive.

In Mednessa, they played sandball with them, dined with them, and some even lived with them. But on that day, it was as if their intertwined histories—going back countless years—didn't exist.

Lucretia rose as usual, ate breakfast with her roommate as usual, and lounged in her bed as usual. The hurried footsteps outside were annoying, but so was her hangover. When those noises intensified into screams and rumbles, she forced herself out of bed and peeked out the window.

Embers glowed, smoke billowed, and fellow humans and elves were stampeding through the street.

Before she could take in the sight further, a member of the city's guard crashed through their wooden door and pushed them outside at spearpoint, mentioning something about an evacuation from their home that was no longer home. He wouldn't let them gather any belongings or even put on street clothes.

The immediacy was for their safety, but being in an elbowing jumble in one's underwear was anything but that.

She was more focused on staying upright than on whatever destination the crowd pushed her toward. Flames crackled and smoke sizzled around them as countless hands and bodies shoved her forward. The woods to the north supplied most of the city's building materials, and the unknown violators had taken full advantage of it.

As for her roommate, Lucretia's eyes had lost track of her the moment they had stepped outside.

Red and orange dominated her vision while the bright rubble around them forced the sweaty crowd so close it became hard to breathe.

In the heat, it hurt to even blink, and her skin felt like it could've melted at any point. Her lips cracked into a bloody mess while painful hacks punished the few breaths she took.

Pop pop pop! Something else set alight, and the sounds layered on top of the flames' clamor.

But... it was all wood, wasn't it? What kind of substance made that kind of noise when burning, and why was everyone falling?

A chill split into her head at that moment, and as warmth rushed out, everything went limp and dark.

When she came to, she was but a floating eye, cursed to watch her fresh body become unrecognizable over several days. A werewolf—perhaps one of the victors—carted her and the rest of the corpses on that street away into a once noble crypt.

There, they scattered their bodies across the underground, not to venerate, but to fit more diseased carcasses far away from any of the conquering heroes. When space became a premium, they hacked apart the remaining corpses and stuffed them into every nook and cranny.

Thankfully, they kept her body whole in the hollow of a stone wall. Lucretia—a mere peasant—liked to think that she had gotten away with some wealthy merchant's resting place.

Days passed, months passed, and years passed as every bit of flesh withered away from her mortal husk. She watched, she counted, and she mourned until the ocean of time diluted the meaning behind those acts into nothingness.

Above, a new civilization emerged, literally on top of their bodies, and life began anew for those who were victorious.

As for below...

Not even the former city spared so many guards for the dead here. Maybe the surge was to keep the acts committed that day a secret, so every new generation could bury them deeper until all was forgotten.

Another night passed in the sea of eternity.

The guards' torchlights refused to stray more than a few meters from their wielders, leaving only a few pockets of light in the underground as they muttered in some unknown tongue. Numbing winds wept through every crack of the catacombs, shushing their footsteps.

Things were as somber as usual.

Lucretia must have memorized every patrol route by now, but it wasn't like she had anything better to do. Like a leaf in a pond, her consciousness just sort of drifted over the cracked pile of bones that had once been her.

She could watch, and do... not much else.

Was this the afterlife for those who acted neither valiant nor vile during their lives? If so, why did only she remain?

Surely others in the deceased crowd lived lives just as unremarkable as hers. Maybe spirits couldn't see each other.

After thousands of pleas over the years, someone must've heard her complaints and taken pity on her today, for a hum broke her thoughts as the guards' sounds faded.

Lucretia felt floatier than usual, and she soared upward, dispersing through the ceiling and ascending through the barren streets of the city. There, her spirit flew toward the starless midnight sky.

Took them long enough.

Finally, she would have her freedom from that damned crypt and join the land without tears. She gazed high at the divine sight denied from her until now, and not down at her desecrated home.

They would remember her, right? Maybe they were waiting for her, too. Sure, a few years had passed, but it was a timeless place. There would be so much to catch up on, from her to everybody and from everybody to—

Fo hrl sglmheg'i nbb... fnjd hrni iepb he anjl... The voice had an unsettling depth.

Just like that, the beautiful scenery above her disappeared.

Lightning crackled into her consciousness, gorging her with knowledge beyond the heaviest tomes in the palace's library. In a fraction of a second that somehow felt like forever, it spoke of a new purpose, of a new allegiance, and of a new life, allowing for no contest.

Her world crashed into a blur as the sky became out of reach once more.

Her front smacked the stone floor of the crypt, and the resulting chill slammed her back against a bone-ridden wall. Like the ground, it sent goosebumps all over her. As her arms flattened her bosom, her shivers rattled the wall.

That was a sensation she didn't miss.

The suffocating dark of the crypt receded, and a silhouette on the opposite wall faded into view. The halls were narrow, barely enough for two people to walk side by side, and the shadow held something shiny.

And sharp.

While shielding her stomach with her arms, Lucretia sprung to her feet. Two clacks rang through the crypt, one after the other.

Her chest felt heavier, balanced by an equally heavy tail and a pair of large batlike wings protruding from her back. The edges of two horns decorated the shivering corners of her vision, and an amber hue flushed her cheeks and the sides of her nose.

Lucretia's skin had taken on a subdued violet tone that ran down to her thighs before darkening. Where it neared her feet, it twisted into blackened fur and a pair of rattling hooves.

There was a weight to her ears with each shiver, and a graze of her fingers confirmed that those had grown longer. They were almost...

Elflike.

And right before her was the equally sharp-eared perpetrator. A dust elf bearing dark brown hair and skin like the rest of his kind.

His knife raised, and she gritted her teeth.

Her leg moved on its own and a muffled thud sounded, followed by an echoing clang. The impact left him in a coughing fit as he rose to a sitting position and stared at her with widened red eyes.

Scary red eyes that never fit the book-buried elves at the library, or the ones who eyed the ground as they passed her on the street. At last, she had met one who looked and acted the part.

So this was the refuse who had brought her back from the dead, and into one of those *things* too...! She stepped closer to the elf and drew a deep breath.

What in the world was that scent?! The sweetness grazed her nostrils, smelling like dessert. A delicious, irresistible dessert.

Lucretia's abdomen cried out in pain as she breathed in again, and her exhale uncovered just how empty she was. If only she could fill that void with something.

A drop of saliva broke into her chest and thoughts. And another. Then another. As she swallowed the excess spit, her thumb swept the trail off her chin.

Drip drop, drip drop. Now they somehow hit the ground instead. She ran her fingers down her body. Dry, dry, dry, dry...

Ooh.

Lucretia shuddered as the digit slicked through her dribbling nethers. Of all the places her body could have pumped blood to... but there was a purpose to it.

The succubus clacked one of her hooves against the ground, and the elf's eyes jumped back up to her gaze.

As she drank in his details, more and more blood rushed to her loins as a hunger unified her mind and body.

Minor as it was in the grand scheme of things, this was what her instincts demanded of her, and regardless of her hunger, he also needed judgment for choosing to bring a lion into this world and not the lamb he had so hoped.

What was he thinking? Didn't he know what a succubus could do, especially to such a fresh and vulnerable elf? Lucretia licked her lips.

Maybe she didn't deserve paradise after all.

She squatted down onto the elf's thighs as her mouth and folds leaked in tandem, tarnishing his pants. Her hands grabbed his wrists, pinning them above his head and against the wall.

The succubus scooted closer to the elf, letting his sugary breath mingle with hers. A bump in his soaked pants stopped her advances.

Fear and lust, but mostly fear, watched as she magically dissolved his clothing. After raising her hips, she lined her slit up with his member before lowering onto him with a growl.

His hands gripped hers back as the distance closed, and the first contact of their nethers jerked his arms out of her hold.

His arms rounded her torso, and he hugged their bodies closer. His moans wet her cleavage, and their spittle merged between the cleft before it continued down their bodies. She, too, moaned as the sticky heat trickled over her clit and into her folds.

"S-so good..." he whispered as his cock slid into her shameful hole.

The bastard wanted it too? And right after she kicked the shit out of him...

What a slutty elf.

But who could've blamed him? Hardly a mortal man or woman could've resisted having their souls ravaged by such a perfect being. That's just how things were.

She wanted him to remember. To remember the bountiful body, unbelievably tight flesh, and otherworldly motions that claimed him first, second, third, fourth, fifth, and beyond, that no she-elf could ever mimic.

Amidst a shared trickle of juices and moans, she hilted him, smothering the elf's thighs with her plentiful rear. The demoness's arms wrapped around the elf's back as her hips rolled, releasing more of the honeyed scent and banishing the crypt's chill.

It didn't take long for his moans to grow loud. Dangerously loud. To where her breasts could no longer shush that noise.

Sheesh, he was definitely thinking with that lower brain there.

She closed her eyes and tried her best to ignore the fingernails bloodying her back. "Shhh... not a peep. The guards might find us."

Lucretia felt a nod against her skin as his breath continued to burn a hole in her chest.

"Good elf. Now give me everything. I'm starving."

As his hips matched her rolls, his cock quivered within her, spewing plenty of pre into her feasting insides while a familiar tingle gathered on her clit, spiking with every one of his thrusts.

Their lunges matched one last time as Lucretia bit her tongue. Their bodies tensed together, and her arms nearly squeezed the life from the elf.

Then she felt it.

That telltale twitch.

2

Heat

"Yes, let it all out..." she mumbled.

The croaks, chirps, and gurgles of the moonlit lake greeted Lucretia as she roused from her dream. Grass tickled her back while the glow of a mooned and starlit sky adorned her front.

What a beautiful, innocent place. Almost.

Shlorp, shlorp, shlorp.

Hundreds of tiny tendrils slithered in and out of her folds as the bulbous tip on her tail sucked on her entrance like a mouth. While they mindlessly thrashed against her slick and tender walls, her moans echoed through the forest clearing for nobody to hear.

Hopefully.

She loosed a breath, and her juices drenched the tentacles. The tail's maw consumed everything on the appendages' slippery retreat, keeping the grass pure for now.

Lucretia's hand snaked down her violet body, grazing across the heart-shaped rune on her abdomen before scaling her smooth mound. Her fingers tested the bulb's suction for a moment. She grunted as her digits popped inside and toyed with the nub that the tentacles had pardoned for far too long.

While the succubus's abdomen hollowed from the touch, her other hand kneaded a perfect breast. Every fondle poured its flesh between her fingers as her work traveled deep. Beads of sweat smeared across the demoness's chest and the watery sheen made its endowment even more noticeable.

Soon, the air filled with a hypnotic taint that drowned her lungs with every breath. Pure beings, vile beings—it didn't matter. One whiff could have turned even the holiest nun into a dripping wreck.

After swallowing a flood of drool, she thrashed her heavy wings until the pristine scent of the lake and forest returned. A long drag of air brought back just enough clarity.

When she concentrated on a sensitive spot within, the bulb's appendages thrust against the rough walls beneath her demonic marking. Each drive against the area jittered her hips toward the shimmered sky as Lucretia's fingers circled her clit, leaving a wet trail in their wake.

"Haaah… almost there…!"

Lucretia's horns gored the vegetation below as her cries reached for the heavens.

She sucked in a breath.

The hand working on her clit slammed into her pelvis, crushing the grinding tentacles against that special spot and forcing her juices through the tangle. Not a droplet escaped the bulb as it devoured its prize.

Waves formed along her tail, traveling toward her body, and Lucretia's belly rumbled as it received the come. Her very own. Her stomach, like all stomachs, digested the fluids anyway, and warmth flowed from the organ to every corner of her reddening body.

Her haunches thrust violently into the air as the succubus's wings flared out with every wave of bliss. Lucretia fanned her fingers across the fragile nub as the other set squeezed a few heated trickles out of a breast. The pale drips ran down her ribcage, joining with several beads of sweat as they fell together into the grass.

The demoness's pussy clamped onto the tendrils, wringing them for all they had. Each pulse drew them deeper, straining her insides while they filled her out. As they bottomed out against the entrance to her womb, her hooves curled and her eyes shut.

Finally, the last delightful crest passed, and her breathing slowed. Her limbs splayed out on the warmed turf as the insects' and water's song returned. In the afterglow, the tentacles at her cervix lazily explored the taut yet tender flesh there—a lovely sensation that shivered her with every blissful spike.

It was perfect. Almost. Nothing could have replaced the real thing.

A pulsing length. The trembling body beneath. Her womb feasting on sweet, innocent seed…

Her tongue swept the saliva off her lower lips. *That* would have been perfection, but this was as good as it would get for tonight. As a summoner's familiar, starving to death wasn't possible, but where was the fun in being painfully empty all the time?

Lucretia's breaths were deep as she brushed her black hair out of sight. Despite her tail's best efforts to drink the evidence, the soil reeked of demonic climax, and no amount of fanning could've hidden her work.

Sweat matted her body and sin drenched her loins.

The succubus bent over and clutched her thighs while the bulb continued to feed. After biting her tongue, she gripped the organ and pulled.

The tendrils stretched her exhausted folds as she made a poorly silenced moan. A bit more pressure split her wide open, and they slurped out before her tail whipped onto the ground.

Come scattered into the lake in front of her like rain while the squirming flesh receded into her tail's maw. The bulb rippled and gurgled as it scarfed down the last of its demonic supper.

"Mrgggh...!"

Lucretia's abdomen, wings, and tail convulsed as another climax took over, and her pussy clutched at the emptiness within, grasping for anything and getting nothing.

While she gritted her teeth, warm fluids gushed out of her pussy and tail, coating the already sticky grass as her hips arched into the air. Her quaking form flung sweat everywhere.

There was definitely no hiding her work now.

After taking a deep breath, she rose, stumbling and nearly falling over. Just the grinding of her thighs was enough to force another gasp and humiliating trickle out of her. It ran down Lucretia's leg and into her formerly fluffy fur.

The succubus made it to the lake's edge before a pair of glowing eyes ambushed her from the water.

She fell back onto the squishy grass with a less impressive gasp. A few blinks later, she scrambled back on all fours to the lake's edge for a closer look.

And the eyes were still there! Amber irises and slit pupils, with sclerae as black as... hers.

Oh.

Maybe a bath would clear things up.

3

Bystander

Water pooled at her hooves, and wind whistled through her curvaceous frame as Lucretia twisted her long hair and fanned her wings. But in the humid air, she could only do so much.

She swept her dripping hair back, and the wet locks punished her with a regrettable slap, shivering her and sending droplets everywhere.

A snap of her fingers unfurled a red-violet ribbon across her left horn, which tied neatly into a bow on its own, and another snap clad her in an ebon robe. The cloth pressed into her skin as she swayed, erasing the remnants of her bath.

It was a garment made just for her, with holes in the hood for her horns, holes in the back for her wings, and a generous amount of space in the front for her breasts. It flowed to her lower calves, keeping her free of any dress code violations at the Coven's hideouts.

For less accepting places, she needed to keep her horns, wings, and tail tucked inside her robe, and button up those extra slits, making those accommodations less useful and things more cramped.

The Coven's advice was to cut those identifying features off. They'd regenerate whenever she'd want them to, and she'd only need to hide her skin and hooves afterward. Of course, that sounded really painful, and Lucretia had yet to do her pain tolerance training.

It was also a shame that Mednes—err, Stygia was off limits. But if the former human stayed dead, she wouldn't be going anywhere, so there wasn't much to complain about.

She kept the robe's hood down, the sash loose, and the buttons unfastened, leaving a strip of obscenity all the way down. There was no need for modesty here and the cloth needed to dry.

Demonsilk was what the cult called it. A stupid name to her until she wore the robe for the first time. Every step rubbed the unbelievably cozy cloth against her skin, making her tremble for her first few steps.

Now... it was back to sentry duty. Ugh.

Eyes scanned the lake and surrounding trees, ears listened beyond the ambiance, and wings felt for stray winds. Nothing. It was always nothing. As expected from a pond in the middle of the forest in the middle of nowhere.

Then, something delectable dragged through her nostrils.

Huh?

Inhaling the sweet breeze once more, her heart raced and her mouth watered. She had to find the source!

Lucretia blinked as her heartbeat stilled.

Oh yeah, it was an intruder or a curious visitor. And here she thought the trees would've done a good job of snuffing out her voice or scent. Guess not.

She glanced at the motionless tent across the lake. He was definitely enjoying his peaceful rest, and there was no reason it couldn't stay peaceful. It was like what, one lost bandit or an explorer or something?

It was kind of exciting, honestly, but it was important not to fantasize too hard yet. Too many distractions and she'd stay either starved or disappointed. And maybe the intruder wouldn't even have anything for her.

Lucretia slashed a freshly bound dagger at an imaginary foe. Either way, their hidden camp needed to remain hidden.

The grass and dark robe masked her approach as she crept toward the overgrown brush. She took a few deep breaths and the rich smell pierced her again. After a final exhale, she dove through the thicket with a rustle.

There they were.

The distance was short, and the silhouette seemed to know as well, as no sooner did she dart for them did they jump and shriek into a choking fit, bashing their back on a poor tree that was soon to be a cutting board.

"Lucie, it's me!" said the red-eyed figure between coughs.

"Sindy?" Her hooves skidded on the grass as she stopped halfway. "Shouldn't you be asleep in your tent?"

A cool breeze sang through the forest at that moment, shuffling around the leaf cover above and shining moonlight onto his gray linen shirt and black pants. Same as this morning, really? Maybe splurging on her robe wasn't such a good idea.

The elf braced against the tree as he rose, stumbling and panting. His skin was only a tad lighter than his dark brown hair, but it did little to conceal his shame.

Pink tinged his soft face, and his long ears twitched as
he grinned.

"Just doing some maaa—uhh... meditation!" He
wiped his hands on his pants with an awful chuckle
before looking her in the eye.

Lucretia glanced back at the bush. It had a clear view
of the lake from the cover. "As was I, and I *finished*."
Her smirk straightened his back. "Did you *finish* too?
Because you don't look too relaxed!"

"Of course I finished... meditating! And I'm perfectly
calm, can't you tell?!"

The succubus trotted closer with her eyes closed
as she hummed a tune. The scent from before was
stronger than ever as it trickled into her lungs. It came
from the grass and it came from a particular part of him.

When she opened her eyes, only a few paces separated
them.

His hand produced a black coil of magic. "Stay back!"

"I'm not mad at you." Lucretia traced his gaze to her
hand. "Oh." The dagger faded away and now she was
the one making an awful laugh.

After a frown and a breath from him, his spell
vanished just as she closed the distance.

Her hand braced against the tree, and she leaned
down to him. "Meditating's so hard on your own..."
Their eyes met. "What if... we did it together?" The
succubus's breaths stuck to his face like glue as her lips
curled into a fangy grin.

Another chilling wind whistled through the thicket,
rustling the canopy above. The branches cracked as a
few shriveled leaves drifted down.

His eyes grew wide for a moment before he swallowed. "Trying to drain more of my life with this... act...? How cruel of you." His voice was low as he clenched his fists.

Lucretia cocked her head, and her fingers twiddled the ribbon on her horn. "Only if I will it. Why would I want that?" Her eyebrows raised as her smile faded away.

"Did you forget what you did to me in that crypt?"

"I was hungry, and you enjoyed it! I think."

"And what happened after that, Lucretia?! You said and did something to me after that!" He walked around her, looking away as his body tensed. "I'm going back to bed. Goodnight."

One step from her was all it took for Alsindor's ears to twitch as he twisted to face her with bared teeth. "Thought you could get me from behind?!" Energy crackled through his arm as another coil gathered in his hand.

Not that terrible sorcery again.

The succubus clutched her arms tight to her chest while gloss coated her eyes, and a blink sent some of it down her cheeks. Her body slumped and swayed, looking like it could've collapsed from the slightest breeze.

His pose stayed firm. "Crying to lower my guard, how—!"

"Alsindor!" Lucretia spoke with a strained voice as her heart pounded. "I did horrible things that day. And I promised to do worse things to you after." Her chest heaved. "Because of that, you've had to worry whether each day would be your last..."

The succubus blinked faster.

"...but you don't need to worry anymore!" Her tears freed and dripped down her chin, falling onto her chest and streaming down as her body shook. "It's wonderful being alive, and I'm alive because of you!"

The elf bore no resistance as she lifted him up and into her robe. Nor did he complain when her hulking wings joined the hug. Within their little shared world, their watery eyes met with faint smiles.

"I really should have told you sooner. Thank you..." she whispered.

A stray tear from the succubus plopped onto his cheek, and she hugged him tighter, pushing his wet face into her neck and flattening her breasts against his chest. The coil of magic fizzled out once more as his hands ran across her bare back to return the hug.

The growing warmth stilled her heart, and her tears spilled onto the elf, joining with his as the glow streaked down their forms.

Everything felt right at that moment.

Their bodies had drifted to the ground as the tears dried and the night marched on. Inside her wings and robe, the embrace continued for what seemed forever.

"You've been so good to me." Lucretia flashed Alsindor a tempting grin as her hand moved lower. "And I know just how to make it up to you."

He grabbed her hand with a frown. "It's still illegal."

"Only to keep you poor elves from going extinct." She ran her fingers through his short hair before flicking an ear and tensing him. "I'm open to sharing you to keep that from happening." His grip weakened, and her hand slipped out. "Come on, you'll love it."

"My mouth..." As she dragged her lips across the same ear, he shivered.

Lucretia pulled his hands to her chest and squeezed. "My breasts..."

"My hands..." Finally, her hand squeezed his inner thigh as another moved down to his waist. Her fingers prowled into his waistband and traced the growing bulge in his underwear.

The succubus grinned at his strained face and blew a breath into it. "And my—"

Alsindor's shaking hands grabbed onto her arm as she flitted along his sensitive underside. Soon her entire hand thrust in and her fingers coiled around his cock through the cloth.

As it throbbed in her grip, she gave it a few quick strokes before he trembled and squeezed her arm.

"Aaaah!"

She stilled her motions and giggled. "Getting close?"

"Your fingers... they're..."

"Just fingers." Lucretia licked her lips. "Don't you want to experience the rest of me?"

His flexing cock was all the answer she needed.

A friendly shove brought his back against the grass, and the succubus crawled toward him as he scooted back at the same pace...

...into that tree with a crack. All he had time for was a blink, and it was all over.

Pouncing on him was easy, and prying his legs open was easier. She rested her head in his lap, savoring the potent scent as her dampened hair streaked his once dry pants.

"So what do you say, Master?"

"I..." He tugged his shirt collar. "Uh..."

4

Taste

Lucretia laid on her stomach, prone on the grass while her legs and tail danced in the air. As her head turned in his lap to face his bulge, Alsindor flicked a leaf off the succubus's head.

After resting a finger on the tip, she leaned in closer to his covered cock. "So hard and we haven't even started." The demoness looked up at him. "You've wanted this for some time, haven't you?" His face grew red as she pressed her cheek against his member. "Naughty Sindy..."

"You're so noisy at night." He panted at her while his hands scrunched the grass underneath. "And your body, the smell, everything... I couldn't take it anymore!"

"And I couldn't take it either. I need to do it with someone else, you know that?" Her cheek nudged his cock again.

Alsindor twisted an ear as he glanced away. "How, umm—"

"Shhhh... let your succubus take care of you."

With a snap of her fingers, their clothes disintegrated and reformed into a neat pile near the bush. Before his hands could finish covering himself, Lucretia snatched them and offered each a horn. They accepted with a light grip.

She eyed his faint abs. Were all elves built this gracefully? His body had not too much muscle as to be brutish, but it still had plenty to satisfyingly dominate. Eventually it would be pinned and ridden beneath her, with its strength conquered and its prize claimed.

The bare cock in front of her stood upright, pulsing every so often. A bead of pre trickled down the underside of its head and collected where it met the foreskin, begging to be lapped away.

He fit perfectly between the forks of her tongue, and while the individual tips licked Alsindor on both sides, his hips shivered as his hands tightened on her horns. A muted sweetness drew from his glans to her tongue, which she lapped to the sound of elven moans until the taste was no more.

After retreating her tongue, she winked at him as his tensed arms dragged her head closer. "That's the spirit, Sin—!"

His next motion spread her lips over his cock, grazing her fangs and tongue across the sensitive, shivering flesh. *Elves are so weak-willed.* The succubus's thoughts drifted to him. *A few licks turned you into a slut.*

Her arms bound his waist as she pulled him closer.

"All this teasing... You asked for it!" Alsindor shook her head by the horns, instantly regretting it with a moan.

She wrapped her lips beneath his glans, and sucked and sucked until her lips slid to the base of his cock, scraping it against her tastebuds as he bucked into her. He squeezed her horns and sweetened her tongue with another bead.

Her demonic tongue looped across the head of his
cock and coiled down, making him groan again as her
wet flesh wrapped around every inch of his leaking
member. The resultant spittle trailed down his shaft
before soaking his balls.

She pumped her length around his oozing shaft like a
spring before her tip slithered down his base and lapped
at his sack. It clenched and rewarded her mouth with
more honey.

"Lu—uaah!" Alsindor's hands pushed on her horns,
and his breaths were quick. "You're—Ah!—g-going too
fast!"

What's wrong, Sindy? As her tongue stroked him, she
gazed up into those pleading eyes of his. *I thought I was
asking for it.*

His fingernails dug into her horns as her tongue
strangled his cock. Her tongue worked him faster,
loosening his hands' grip as he continued to leak, and
his back muscles contracted against her probing fingers.

After uncoiling her tongue, she lifted her head to
suck on his dripping cockhead a few times before she
enveloped his member again to milk him. His hands
loosened with each draw until they fell to her sides.

Another draw forced out a cry.

As his hips bucked, Lucretia's mouth and hands
withdrew from him as her arms wrapped around his
thighs. A jerk of his body peeled him off the tree, leaving
him flat against the grass. She hoisted his thighs over her
shoulders, keeping his lower half raised and confused.

The elf gawked at the succubus as his cock rose and fell
with his breaths. After fogging the head with her whiffs,

she lowered her lips upon him again while admiring his pleasured face.

She engulfed just his tip and drank.

"I... ahh! Uaaaah!" Alsindor's cries echoed through the forest as his hands tore the grass.

Her eyes widened.

Pleasure echoed through her as his cock twitched, and a stream of juices flowed out of her, bathing her loins in heat as Lucretia's hips thrust into the ground.

She buried her fingernails into his thighs while the motions grazed her clit against a blade of grass. Soon, the hardened nub twitched in tandem with his cock.

So that's how it worked. Shame she had no more time to ponder over it.

Her cheeks hollowed as they wrung the sweet ooze from him. It went down just as quickly, coating her mouth and throat with a delightful aftertaste that demanded more.

And more she would have.

Lucretia sucked out another thick bolt. Then another. And another. And another. His cock would pulse and she would suck at that exact moment, forcing the gooey feast through his shaft and into her lapping tongue and stomach.

How kind of Alsindor to save so much for her! His seed flooded her mouth with every twitch and thrust, staying generous as she drank her fill amidst his blissful cries. Only when she felt full did the treat diminish to a trickle, and then to a drop.

When the pulsing stopped, she pursed her lips under its softening head and pulled away as he cried out. A pop freed his stretched member and released a final helping of come.

It was so much sweeter and thicker than the rest as she chewed and passed it around her mouth. After dropping his thighs, she climbed over him to meet his face before gulping noisily with a smile. The sweetness clung to her mouth afterward, diminishing slowly from her continued swallows.

The world started spinning, and an infectious warmth sloshed in her belly as red crossed her face. It had been long since she had last fed. Too long.

Lucretia's tongue dabbed the corner of her lips, and she burped loudly, making the elf flinch. "Aren't you just delicious?"

"Where did you learn that?!" he asked between breaths.

"A succubus just knows." She lowered her face to his and licked a trail of drool off his chin. "Do you think an elf girl could do better?"

Alsindor rolled his eyes.

Her upper arms squeezed her breasts together. "Admit it. I'm better in every way."

After spreading her thighs, she smothered his groin with her rear and wiggled her hips, smearing her juices all over his member as they both squirmed from the initial contact. "And I'll prove it again."

He frowned at her. "I wouldn't age a few years from fucking another elf."

"I would never!" Lucretia crossed her arms under her bust and pouted as her ears drooped. "You trust me, don't you?"

The elf looked away.

"Come on Sindy. I was weak and angry back then, and what's a few years to an elf if I can't resist the urge again?" Okay, maybe she should've left that last part out.

The succubus rolled one of her pointed ears between her fingers and sighed. "Well... if you don't want to, then we won't."

"Giving up already?" The elf's eyes danced around her gaze before focusing on her. "Maybe you can suppress your instincts after all, and I'll be fine."

"I like you and familiars die without a host, so it's in my emotions *and* instincts to keep you around. For as long as possible." A strand connected their sexes as she reclined. "I suppose you'd also feel safer if I'm on the bottom..."

"Oh, about that. I'd rather umm, you... be on top." He coughed and made a shaky grin at her. "You know, b-because you're... the expert here! And I could totally fight you off should the need arise, no problem!" Black crackled in one of his palms for a moment.

"I really have ruined you." She licked her lips, and they curled into a smirk. "Not that I'm complaining. I've always wanted to do this to you with more... cooperation."

Damn it, that also sounded so much better in her head. Oh well.

Her tail tip prodded his softened cock as it spewed tendrils onto him. They wormed and coiled over the base of his shaft before aligning his flimsy length with her hole.

Alsindor flinched as his hands hesitated. "What the hell are *those*?!"

"Shouldn't you know, Coven demonologist? That's what you get for reading about succubi instead of fucking one, bookworm." She stuck out her tongue.

"I've had you for only a week!" His ears twitched.

"That's one hundred fifty hours of fucking we haven't done."

"Actually, it's sixty-ei—Aiiieee!" He made a cute cry as his shaft prodded the succubus. He didn't sink any deeper than that, but the contact alone was enough for a mutual shiver.

Her juices flowed down his shaft, and a shift of her hips kneaded his pre into her slit as he slid deeper. All she had to do now was relax, and the feeding would begin.

"Not yet! I'm still sensitive!" The elf's hands rushed to his groin and her hands snatched them. By now, just the grip of her folds was enough to keep his member up, so her tail pulled away.

She dragged the elf's hands above his shoulders before slamming his wrists into the grass. Alsindor didn't resist, but then again, he wanted answers, not a fight. If he truly wanted to, he'd use that spell again, and she'd be a pile of ashes.

"I know that! I'm the expert here, remember?" Her muscles softened just enough for his cockhead to slip inside her, and her wings splayed as they shared twists and whines.

His hands struggled against her hold. "T-then let me rest!"

"I *will* let you rest." She freed his hands and braced hers near the sides of his head as she leaned into him. Her bosom jumped inches from his avoidant gaze while she flicked his ear and flashed him a sad look. "Didn't we just talk about trusting each other?"

His face was flushed as he stared down at their linked bodies. Then he met her eyes and sighed. "Just take it slow."

She took a deep breath and whispered, "I'll be as gentle as I can." His hands grasped her wrists as she lowered her hips and fully relaxed her muscles. Inch by inch, her insides claimed him until her clit pressed into his pelvis.

She ground her nub against his skin, which felt a lot like demonsilk. Was demonsilk actually made from…? Nah.

"Hnngh!" His grip tightened on Lucretia's arms as he bucked against her overwhelming thighs.

The tendrils had filled her more thoroughly, but there was something that felt *right*—taking a proper cock. She peeled her hand away from his grip and brought it to her lower abdomen. It was burning. While her palm applied pressure, his length flexed against her diminished insides before its curvature brushed against a rough patch.

"It hits everything in me. No wonder elf girls are always smiling." Her free hand returned to tug at his ear. "Maybe I should keep you for myself." She giggled as his abs tensed.

Her motions had split her hair down to her sides, and a shake of her head passed most of it to her front, where it dipped down and shrouded his peripheral vision.

He was too busy ogling her chest to notice. A flick of his ear fixed that, and he turned to her dampened strands right away.

"I don't mind if you stare." She swayed her torso and her breasts did the same. "Quite fuller than an elf's, wouldn't you say?"

He had no answer.

She closed her eyes and thought of the soft cock inside her, and her muscles fluttered up and down his shaft. Her tunnel clutched his sensitive tip, sparing it from her preying flesh as more pre dripped from him. Her walls massaged it into their increasingly slimy coating.

The elf's hardening length contracted every so often as her liquid arousal flooded over him and seeped out of her. It drained onto his taut balls and stuck to him like syrup.

"Feeling better?" Lucretia looked down and the elf's head tilted up to her.

His semirigid cock sprung within her. "You're…" A moan escaped his lips. "…amazing." Another squeeze from Lucretia raised his shaking hands. They ran over her sides and to her back, cupping her shoulder blades as they pulled her body down.

He hugged her so close that her cleavage enveloped his face. Along with his warm skin, drool smeared against her breasts, adding to their sweaty coating. Soon, his gasps were fogging and tickling her sternum with every nuzzle from her folds.

"Couldn't resist, could you?" She shook her chest again, mashing her bosom against him. "Elven bee stings just can't compare."

Lucretia tensed her abdomen and swirled her hips, running his cock across the meager walls and grazing him against more sensitive plots of flesh. As their bodies quaked, her hole stiffened and their motions strained his dripping head against those sweet spots once more. Now she was the one digging her fingers into the grass.

His nails indented her back as they moaned in unison.

She steadied her waist and flexed her pussy against his cock. One moment she'd be tight, and the next moment she'd be loose. Tight, loose, tight, loose. His fidgeting hands held the succubus close as the rhythms nursed his member back to life. It beat as it spilled healthy streaks of pre into her that mixed with her own.

She teased him with another squeeze. "Does Master want more?"

Alsindor's cheeks were on fire while his breath seared her bust. "Yes…" After he released his hug with a shlick, he inhaled the cool air and coughed.

She breathed in as well. Their elven and demonic scents blended into a vile aura that cursed the natural order. Unlike him, she could breathe it in all day, and every gasp made her mouth, pussy, and tail leak in tandem.

As she rose, a wet sheen coated her cleavage, and flecks of sweat sparkled their bodies. With another bounce of her breasts, she leaned back and gripped his thighs with her hands. He swallowed and blinked as his hands went back to fiddling with the vegetation.

Her wings raised to the skies and tensed.

Her body rose, aided by an updraft, and his member ground against her lustrous insides on the ascent. As gravity slammed her back onto his cock, he slid against her walls again.

"Haah!" The sinners' cries wove together as her nails dug into his thighs. Their chests heaved and their hips danced.

He winced at their bonded waists. "You're so… tight…!"

"Tighter than any elf." She squeezed him again. "Do you like how it molds to fit you perfectly?"

Alsindor shot her another frown before closing his eyes, and she raised her wings and slammed down again. The elf's spewing member choked her folds, marking it with a clingy warmth as his lower body shuffled.

She drove her wings faster and faster, needing more of that delightful fluid in her. Each hilt slathered her clit against his equally delightful skin as the melded liquids splashed out of her and stained their haunches.

Lucretia looked down. His eyes were back to gorging on her lively breasts. A lovely sight for her, as it was for him.

Her hole contracted on its descent and her spittle ran down her chest in a bubbly trail as their bodies burned.

The elf's gaze jumped to their nethers. "It's scary how *not wrong* this feels." He chuckled.

"It's only natural." Her motions stilled. "A succubus and her master are meant to take care of each other. That's why our orgasms are linked."

"Linked?" His eyes grew wide. "So that's why I've been waking up sticky."

"Oh Sindy, for a know-it-all, you sure know absolutely nothing about succubi." She grunted and renewed her cadence. "There's so much I need to teach you."

She flashed her fangs.

5

Feast

Wet smacks and sharp exhales breached the forest's ambiance.

Just one hand was enough to pin both of his above his head, and his body writhed as she pounded her rear into his groin.

Lucretia's stilled wings had fanned out to their sides, drooping into the tickling undergrowth. Her wing bases were a tender red and her legs motioned in their place. The mouth on the succubus's flailing tail slobbered each time she sheathed him, scattering her juices across the forest floor.

She brought her free hand to her mouth and popped the thumb inside. Her tongue lathered it until it glistened with spittle. With a string still connecting it to her lips, she pulled it away from her mouth and toward his. The wet digit prodded at his lips before forcing its way through, squeaking against his clenched teeth.

"Come on, it's sweet. And you'll last longer too," she said.

His teeth clattered for a moment before forming a gap. The succubus's thumb entered and twisted across his tongue until none of her spittle remained.

He closed his lips around the digit and swallowed.

When he opened his mouth, she dragged her thumb to a corner, hooking his cheek from within. His ear protruded between her middle and ring fingers as they gripped the side of his face and tugged at his mouth, coating her fingers in fresh saliva.

"How do I taste?" she asked.

He answered with a gurgle.

"That's what I thought." Her pussy grew taut while it sprang faster on him, and the glides across her excited folds turned into scrapes as their bodies pleaded for release.

He gulped down the excess spit between his gurgling pants while his hands balled into fists. The elf's wrists arched against her hold as he answered each crash of her hips with a buck of his own.

"Hnngh... Aaah!" The elf made a particularly hard thrust and his cock flexed inside her drawn hole. A fiery spurt erupted from his tip, branding her suffocating walls in his essence. The succubus's flesh pinned the treat against his glans, and not a drop leaked out.

Lucretia pulsed her muscles over his cockhead and drew the sweet bounty deeper. The warmth eased her aching cervix as her womb sucked and sucked until his fluids kissed her deepest recesses.

It was an emission meant to be sown in an elven womb. Instead, it was trapped in its cruel replica, where its denizens would find no egg as the mockery drained everything from them.

Perhaps they would put up a fight within her, but it was all for nothing. They were mere afterthoughts to his pleasure. First into her stomach, and then into her cradle.

He had cast his seeds so willingly to the slaughter. And slaughter she would.

Millions over and over, to feed one as nature intended.

How it clung to and filled her insides! It felt utterly perfect inside her, whirling in her belly and now her womb. Her heart fluttered as the two distinct heats connected.

While the marking outside glowed, her womb digested the captive liquid. Ecstasy bloomed from the grumbling organ, coursing through her nerves to the tips of her wings, tail, horns... everything.

Adding to the feeling, Lucretia's echoed climax surged up her spine and crashed down to her legs. It shivered her arms, curled her hooves, and painfully flattened the grass with her wings. The succubus withdrew her hands from the elf, bracing them against the ground as her waist continued to make quick plunges onto him.

A familiar aroma held her mind as she held her breath, and drool spilled from her mouth, streaming down her chin. Her tongue slipped out, trying in vain to capture the runaway spittle while it leached down her neck and into her cleavage.

Another thrust filled her with a fresh rope, just as ample as his first. She struggled to steady her trembling walls, so the nectar ran out of her, coating their groins.

Lucretia reeled as her core muscles violently contracted. There was no way to retrieve her tongue, and it dangled and dribbled as she panted. The succubus's arms collapsed, and she laid prone against the elf, drowning him in her breasts. His head tilted as high as it could go, and his equally hot panting relieved her neck.

Alsindor crossed his arms around her back once more. Each one seized the opposite wing base and pulled, forcing his neck deeper into her cleavage.

Slutty elf.

This time, a softer pulse of seed fed her, and she freed her breath. She shut her eyes and focused on his cock again, enjoying the shared sensation. Her lower folds sealed his shaft, while the muscles above his glans siphoned the trapped come into her insatiable womb. She quivered as more of his essence sloshed within her tender walls.

He tugged her wing bases again, mashing their bodies together as his toes curled and tongue flopped out. Meanwhile, her pussy continued to bob on his dribbling yet still stiffened cock.

Finally weighed down by the afterglow, his arms dropped into the grass.

As she leaned back onto the elf's legs, his member shifted in her and she braced herself against his thighs.

She looked down. Their chests and waists gleamed in fluids.

What a mess.

Her hand reached down to their groins, scooping up part of their wasted climaxes. She brought it to her mouth and inhaled the brilliant aroma before lapping herself clean. Combined, it somehow tasted even better.

"Your saliva didn't help at all!" His voice twitched her ears.

"Notice how it doesn't hurt when I do *this*?" Lucretia danced her hips, and the elf cringed for an agony that didn't come. "It kills your waiting period so I can feed on you all night." She smirked at him with half-lidded eyes. "If you want…"

Her cleansed fingers ran against her groin, leaving a path of spit on her now dimmed sigil. The womb underneath felt much lighter now.

Alsindor groaned as he braced his hands against the ground and lifted his torso. "When I said I wanted to sleep, I wasn't lying."

"I'll give you the sweetest of dreams, then." Her digits traced from the base of his cock up to her clit.

His cock shuddered as her fingers worked their come into her nub and hood.

She rose slowly, and both grunted and flinched as his length shlicked and popped out of her. Liquid ran down her thighs, drenching the fur at her ankles before it could pool in the grass.

After scooping the limp elf into a bridal carry, she walked toward the bush and lake.

Their splash broke the gleaming tension of the water as the chilling liquid consumed their shivering bodies. A few bubbles later and they resurfaced.

"H-hey! I can wash myself!"

"Oh, I'm sorry. I thought you were sleepy."

6

Dream

The tent was so much bigger on the inside, and so much darker, too. Thankfully, the glow of her eyes and the dying candle kept things from being completely black.

Her arms wrapped across his shoulders and chest in an X, squeezing his back into her front. As for her, a pillow kept her head propped atop the soft bedroll.

The succubus would be his bed for tonight.

Each jostle shook his wet hair, drawing trails above her breasts. His motions tickled her as well, and her back shuffled against the damp cloth. Her own watery hair ran down her sides to her hips, leaving dark streaks on the bedroll.

"What do you think?" Her long tongue snared one of his fidgeting ears.

He swallowed before continuing to stare at the monstrosity in front of him. "S-s-so g-good..."

"I figured," she said, freeing his ear.

Her tail's writhing bulb had latched onto his cock tight as hundreds of tiny tendrils writhed against it, covering his member in hot mucus. The bulb pulsated over his length as it fed on his pre, and not a trickle escaped the flared entrance's suction.

After giving his ear another lick, she prodded his slit with a fleshy hair and whisked away a drop.

"Hnngh!"

She giggled. "Close again? This should finish you." Her arms mashed his heated body against hers, and her legs twisted over his before spreading them out.

The tail's hairs became frenzied and his hands grasped her arms. The soft writhes from prior turned into powerful thrusts around his member as his thighs jostled against hers. While the elf arched and jerked upward fruitlessly, he sucked in a deep breath and looked up at her.

Lucretia smiled at his labored face and calmed the tendrils. "Don't resist, just let it happen." She dragged her hands across his and gripped them tight. "It'll feel so much better that way." She rippled the bulb again with a grunt.

He nodded at her before closing his eyes and calming his breaths.

"That's it..." she whispered. "Let me take care of everything..."

As his cock beat softly, his come melted into her. The tendrils soon flew into a furor, sweeping every drop from his tip and fanning their spoils into the tail's depths. One curious tendril flicked beneath his glans over and over while the others coiled over his member, wringing out more dollops of seed.

Small, delectable waves rippled through her tail toward her body, and her abdomen contracted as she clung to him. The succubus's arms clutched inward, driving him so deep into her cleavage that her breasts muffled his ears. White oozed from her nipples and she gathered the fluid onto her fingertips. His mouth cleaned them nicely.

Their groins thrust up in unison as her insides flexed.

She gritted her teeth and concentrated on the fever gushing out of her. Just before it ruined the bedroll, it dissipated and splashed into the lake outside.

Leaks became drips and slurps became sips as the pulpy hairs slowed to a gentle massage. Her legs untwisted from the elf's, but the rest of his bindings remained.

Sweat glistened their forms, forming a gluey mess where their skin touched.

Like the forest outside, the tent now reeked of sin, and their efforts in the lake had become undone. Maybe they should have slept outside.

Too late now. Lucretia stretched her limbs and yawned.

Summons like her didn't need to sleep, so why did she feel like sleeping right now? Maybe it'd be okay to skip the rest of sentry duty. There weren't that many hours left in the night.

Her muscles relaxed as she joined him in slumber. Most of her, anyway. Her tail continued to caress him as he made mellow thrusts into its bulb. Hopefully, it'd stay attached to him until morning.

A fan of her wings put the candle out of its misery, and as her dimming eyes closed, she squeezed his hands again.

All these wonderful things happened in just one night, and there'd be a whole day tomorrow, and plenty more after that...

It was good to be alive.

About the Author

I write erotic fantasy stories featuring monster girls.

Enjoy reading about voracious succubus tails, slime-girl clone harems, fluffy harpy wings, and much, much more. Nothing excites me more than exotic body parts and fantastical abilities being used in naughty ways, especially when there's an assertive monster girl taking charge.

Follow me on these platforms:

Website | cithrel.com

Newsletter | cithrel.com/newsletter

Twitter | twitter.com/cithrel

Goodreads | goodreads.com/cithrel

Join the Newsletter

Join my mailing list to stay updated with what I'm working on: cithrel.com/newsletter

As thanks for signing up, you'll also receive **a free digital copy of *Succubus With Benefits 1.5***, a book that isn't available anywhere else!

The story takes place right after the events of the first book. It features sensual bathing, a hands-on investigation into succubus anatomy, and a very lewd cover illustration.

Also by Cithrel

If you enjoyed the story, consider leaving a review and exploring another monstrous tale. Your support is always appreciated!

A newsletter-exclusive freebie! The day after, a succubus helps her master come to terms with his new desires.

An elf finds comfort in her water elemental. Literally.

A harpy unwinds with the help of her two fluffy servants.

Printed in Great Britain
by Amazon